I0669803

John C. Roe

Some Obscure and Disputed Points in Byronic Biography

John C. Roe

Some Obscure and Disputed Points in Byronic Biography

ISBN/EAN: 9783337388539

Printed in Europe, USA, Canada, Australia, Japan

Cover: Foto ©Raphael Reischuk / pixelio.de

More available books at **www.hansebooks.com**

SOME OBSCURE AND DISPUTED POINTS IN BYRONIC BIOGRAPHY.

INAUGURAL-DISSERTATION

PRESENTED TO THE

UNIVERSITY OF LEIPZIG

FOR THE

DEGREE OF DOCTOR OF PHILOSOPHY

BY

JOHN C. ROE.

LEIPZIG-R.
PRINTED BY OSWALD SCHMIDT
1893.

TO MY FATHER

IN GRATEFUL REMEMBRANCE.

Introduction.

I have persuaded myself, and I think with reason, that writing on certain obscure and unconnected points in Byronic biography is the only profitable proceeding in writing on Byron's life since the publication of Jeaffreson's work 'The Real Lord Byron', which, so far as the sources of information at the disposal of Byronic biographers go up to the present date, has given on the whole a faithful account of the great poet's life, and has displayed much discernment and understanding of human nature in his explanations of the motives of Byron's actions and his descriptions of the poet's friends and surroundings. In fact, there can be no doubt that Jeaffreson's work on Byron, though in some instances inaccurate through the author's evident wish to render his book pleasant reading and popular, is one of the best specimens, if not the best English biographical composition of the present century.

The first complete Life of Byron written after Moore's, that of Galt (*London 1830*[1]), which has been valuable as the first attempt at a relation of the history of the Byron family and for his account of the poet's behaviour on board the Malta packet, of which Galt was an eye witness, is defective in that lack of ability of the biographer (which is characteristic of contemporary biographies on men of genius) to appreciate how much Byron's judgement and intellect was

[1] Published by Colburn and Bentley.

in advance of the world of his time. One of the most startling proofs of the same may be found in the comparison of the modernness of the sentiment and character of the greatest of his productions and the last of his poetical works on which he wrote, Don Juan, with that of English or foreign productions of the first half of the present century.

Sir Cosmo Gordon's 'Life and Genius of Lord Byron',[1] and Iley's 'Life, Writings, Opinions and Times of G. G. Noel Byron etc.'[2] are full of absurdities. The biographies of Lake (1827)[3] and Armstrong (1846) and all other writings on Byron's life which preceeded the publication of the first edition of Trelawny's book (1858) and the first lives of Shelley (*Medwin's 1847, and Lady Shelley's 1859, both full of errors, though giving many facts hitherto unknown*), so far as their authors were not for some time companions or eye witnesses of the poet's doings, as were Galt and Hunt, are worthless for the purposes of critical research, as their authors did not possess the necessary information for accurate composition.

Eberty's work (first edition 1862, 2nd ed. 1879) is in general a repetition of the facts stated in the biographical portion of Moore's 'Life', with a limited use of Galt's book as regards Byron's ancestors, and a few references to Dallas, Lady Blessington, Gamba, Millingen, Bruno, Stanhope, Parry, and in the second edition to Teresa Guiccioli's (then Marquise de Boissy) book; and is little more than a popular exposition of Byron's life, without critical treatment or references.

Elze's biography (1st edition 1870, 3rd 1886) resembles a catalogue of all manner of facts and nonsense, collected with admirable industry from all available sources of information on Byronic biography, and thrown together with

---

[1] London 1824.

[2] London 1825.

[3] Lake's book is a kind of vestpocket edition of Byron's Life, published in Frankfort o/M.

little or no discrimination as to the worth, truth, and character of his witnesses and information. Another prime fault in Elze's book is the total ignorance it displays of the Byronic papers in the library of the British Museum, without a knowledge of which intelligent writing on certain portions of Byron's life is utterly impossible. Take for instance his note to page 188 of the third edition of his work as regards the relations of Lady Byron to Mrs. Leigh after Byron's death (im Jahre 1840 offenbarte sie (*Lady Byron*) Medora Leigh, dass sie eine Tochter ihres Gemahls sei, *und setzte, dessen ungeachtet, allem Anschein nach das freundschaftliche Verhältnis zu ihrer Mutter bis zu deren Tode fort !!!*).

I have noticed Prof. Elze's personal opinions on the points I have written only. Those portions of his work which justified Bleibtreu in calling it a *Klatschgeschichte*, and which touch to a certain extent points on which I have endeavoured to give the results of others investigation, or to throw new light, I have ignored as unprofitable.

Nichol's work (Ist edition 1880) on Byron in the English Men of Letters, though written on a small compass and for the most part not entering into details on the subjects with which I have dealt, is an immense improvement on Elze's book in its generally impartial attitude towards Byron as a man, and more intelligent comprehension of his character.

Jeaffreson's work[1] was first published in 1883 in 2 vols, in 1884 a one volume edition appeared and then the so-called standard edition, the two latter being especially interesting in containing the Byronic papers in the possession of Mr. Morrison, published by Jeaffreson in the Athenæum for August 4th and 18th 1883, besides some crushing remarks on the ignorance and blundering of the reviewers of his book in the "Quarterly" and "Nineteenth Century."

Since the publication of Jeaffreson's book on Byron, the

---

[1] The Real Lord Byron; New Views of the Poet's Life, London, Hurst & Blackett.

only complete biography that has been published on the poet, that of Roden Noel (*London 1890*), is essentially an epitome of Jeaffreson's work, containing nothing new on the subject with the exception of a schoolfellow of Byron's, Lord Jocelyn's (Mr. Noel's grandfather) account of the general character of Byron's behaviour at Harrow.

The only work on the history of English literature that has displayed independent research, and an intelligent conception of the great poet's character, that of Bleibtreu,[1] is excellent in many respects in the purely biographical parts (*besides containing the best literary criticism on Byron's works that has been published up to the present date*) having brought to light and treated independently and judiciously several of the most obvious mistakes in Jeaffreson's work. Bleibtreu's chief weakness is that of all literary historians when not writing exclusively on any single author, that of not possessing all the information procurable and adequate for a critical treatment of the subject. His weakest point however is his lack of knowledge of Shelleyan biography which causes him to make some curious though pardonable mistakes, for instance, his mistaking Jane Williams, wife of Captain Williams who was drowned with Shelley off Via Reggio, for Jane (Claire) Clairmont.[2]

Translations such as that of the Autobiographical portions of Moore's Life of Byron and Byron's letters therein contained by Engel, and biographical prefaces to editions of his works, I have not deemed necessary to mention as they depend solely for their information on biographies of the poet.

Such work as Lady Morgan's Memoirs (London 1864), those of Viscount Melbourne (London 1878), and the ecclesiastically coloured memoirs of Hodgson (1878), and Harness (1871), are interresting, especially the two former, for the

---

[1] Englische Litteratur-Geschichte im 19. Jahrhundert.

[2] Bleibtreu: Englische Litteratur-Geschichte im 19. Jahrh. 2 ed. p. 211.

light they throw on the character of the society and some of the individuals Byron frequented from his arrival in England from his first trip in the Orient, till his final departure from England in the spring of 1816. The memoirs of Hodgson are of minor importance since Jeaffreson's publications in the Athenæum, for strictly critical purposes, though essential for a knowledge of the character of one of Byron's most intimate friends. Harness' 'Life' contains but a few lines referring to Byron.

Kennedy's 'Conversations on Religion'[1] with its appendix, Stanhope's Greece in 1823 and 1824,[2] containing the so-called 'sketch' of Byron printed also in the English translation of Elze's book, Milligen's Memoir on the affairs in Greece,[3] Finlay's 'Reminiscenses' of Byron in his 'History of Greece'[4] and 'History of the Greek Revolution'[5] *(the wording of the part referring to Byron is the same in both works)*, besides the value of their testimony as regards Byron's department in Missolonghi, may be consulted with profit for the different descriptions of the poet's character, which vary in worth; that of the psalm-singing and ignorant Kennedy is doubtless the worst, that of Finlay the best.

Such works as Blaquière's 'Narrative of a second Visit to Greece',[6] De Salvo's 'Lord Byron en Italie et en Grèce',[7] Washington Irving's 'Crayon Miscellany'[8] (Newstead Abbey p. 323—441), Macay's 'Lord Byron at the Armenian Convent',[9] Roger's,[10] and Coleridge's 'Table Talk',[11] and Crabbe

[1] London 1830.
[2]   „   1825.
[3]   „   1831.
[4]   „   1877.
[5]   „   1861.
[6]   „   1825.
[7]   „   · 1825.
[8] Philadelphia 1874.
[9] Venice 1876.
[10] London 1856.
[11]   „   1884.

Robinson's 'Diary'.[1] are of secondary importance. The appendix to the second edition of Hobhouse's 'Travels in Albania'[2] is chiefly valuable as a sketch of Byron's character.

Other and more important sources of information on Byron, such as Trelawny's Records etc. Shelley's letters, and others which I have cited in the following pages I omit mentioning here.

Works on the history of English literature I have deemed unnecessary to cite, as the biographical portions, with the single exception of Bleibtreu's work, are void of independent research.

I have consulted all sources of information on Shelleyan biography extant, but till the 'Shelley papers' are published, if such be ever the case, no important acquisitions to our knowledge may be expected in that direction. The best biographies of Shelley up to the present date are those of Jeaffreson.[3] and Dowden.[4]

The biography of Mrs. Shelley by Mrs. Julian Marshall[5] is highly valuable in containing many hitherto unpublished letters of importance to both Shelleyan and Byronic biographers. One of the most interesting portions of Mrs. Marshall's work is the correspondence which took place after Byron's death between Mrs. Shelley and Claire, and that between Mrs. Shelley and Trelawny.

'Mrs. Shelley' by Lucy Madox Rossetti (London 1890) is but an epitome of Mrs. Marshall's work, although written independently of it.

Review articles on Shelley and other works on him, which I have not found occasion to quote, I shall not mention

---

[1] London and New York 1872.
[2] „ 1855.
[3] The Real Shelley 1885 (Hurst & Blackett).
[4] Percy Bysshe Shelley 1886 (Kegan Paul, French, Trübner & Co.).
[5] The Life and Letters of Mary Wollstoncraft Shelley by Mrs. Julian Marshall, London 1889. 2 vol.

here, as I intend treating of him only so far as he plays a *rôle* in Byronic biography.

The most complete bibliography on Byron's works and life is that of John Anderson of the British Museum, which is published as an appendix to Roden Noel's 'Life of Byron' (London 1890). Others less complete and referring more to the purely biographical portions of writings on Byron, may be found in the 'Dictionary of National Biography' edited by Leslie Stephen, and in the copious notes to the third edition of Prof. Elze's book.[1]

Essays of a more or less literary character on Byron[2] are numerous, but are biographically worthless.

Manuscript Writings.

a) The Byronic Correspondence (British Museum).

b) Byronic writings belonging to Mr. Alfred Morrison.

c) Lady Dorchester's Byronic manuscripts. (Lady Dorchester is the eldest daughter of Hobhouse, Lord Broughton). *unpublished.*

d) Lord Wentworth's papers, *unpublished.*

e) Claire Clairmont's letter to Byron (Egerton Mss. British Museum).

f) Hobhouse papers (British Museum), *unpublished.*

g) The 'Shelley Papers', *unpublished.*

Review Articles of Biographical character.
Academy, Oct. 9, 1869.
„ „ 23, 1875.
„ July 19, 1879.
„ Oct. 26. 1889.

[1] Berlin 1886.
[2] e. g. Macaulay's.

Athenæum, March 27, 1858.
        ,,   Nov.   9, 1861.
        ,,   July   19, 1862.
             Dec.   22, 1866.
        ,,   May   16, 1868.
        ,,   ,,   22, 1869.
             Oct.   9, 1869.
             Nov. 20, 1869.
             ,,   27, 1869.
             Jan.   6, 1872.
             April   5. 1873.
             —   1876, II, p. 306.
             April 27, 1878.
             March 29, 1879.
             April   5, 1879.
        ,,   Dec.   24, 1881.
        ,,   July   15, 1882.
        ,,   Dec.   12, 1882.
             May   12, 1883.
             Aug.   4, 1883.
             ,,   18. 1883.
             May   24, 1884.
             July   5, 1884.
        ,,   Aug.   30, 1884.
        ,,   Sept.   6, 1884.
        ,,   ,,   19, 1885.
        ,,   ,,   26, 1885.
             Oct.   3. 1885.
        ,,   ,,   31, 1885.
             Dec.   5, 1885.
                  19, 1885.
             ,,   26, 1885.
             Jan.   9, 1886.
                  16, 1886.
             ,,   23. 1886.
             May   22, 1886.

Since 1886 no article of biographical character has appeared on either Byron or Shelley in this journal with the single exception of the critique on Mrs. Marshall's book in the Athenæum for Nov. 23, 1889. Ten other articles which have appeared on Shelley, are critiques on editions of his works or on works of a purely character referring to them. Nothing of the nature of literary criticism whatever has appeared in the above mentioned journal since 1886 on Byron.

Academy Oct.   9, 1869.
„   „   23, 1875.
„   July 19, 1879.
„   Oct. 26, 1889.
„   Dec. 12, 1890.

Blackwood's Magazine Aug. 1819.
„   „   Jan. 1822.
„   „   June 1824.
„   „   Jan. 1834.
„   „   July 1869.
„   „   Jan. 1870.
„   „   Feb. 1870.

Revue des Deux Mondes, Dec. 1, 1873.
„   „   „   „   Jan. 15, 1882.

Edinburgh Review, April 1871.
„   „   „   1878.
„   „   Oct. 1882.

Frazer's Magazine June 1858.
„   „   March 1860.

Fortnightly, June 1878.

Lancet, Sept. 20, 1827.
„   June 2, 1883.

Literary Gazette, May 19, 1821.

London Magazine, Oct. 1824.

New Monthly 1830, I.

 ,,   ,,   1835, III.

Nineteenth Century, Aug. 1883.

 ,,   ,,   Nov. 1891.

Notes and Queries, Series I—VII, London 1849.

Quarterly Review, June 1853.

 ,,   ,,   Oct. 1869.

 ,,   ,,   Jan. 1870.

 ,,   ,,   Jan. 1878.

 ,,   ,,   July 1883.

Victoria Magazine, Nov. 1873.

Westminster Review, July 1824.

 ,,   ,,   Jan. 1825.

The Relations of Lord Byron to Robert Southey (Verhältnis von Robert Southey zu Lord Byron), Anglia, III 426.

Herrig's Archiv, Bd. 70, p. 459, Contains a critique of Jeaffreson's book.

SOME OBSCURE AND DISPUTED POINTS IN BYRONIC BIOGRAPHY.

JOHN C. ROE.

Contents.

From Byron's birth (which in spite of what Dallas and several others have said in favour of Dover, most probably took place in No. 24 Holles Street, London, on the 22 nd of January 1788[1] till he became a member of Trinity College, Cambridge, in October 1805, his life is comparatively free from events of vital importance unknown to Byronic biographers. Most individuals who had an important influence on the poet's character are known, at least by name, up to that date.

I.
'Thyrza'.

Referring to his friendship for Edward Noel Long, Byron writes in one of his journals, — "His friendship, and a violent, though pure, love and passion — which held me at the

---

[1] See Add. MS. 31037, p. 7. British Museum. Letter from Byron's mother to Mrs. Leigh (wife of General Leigh, residing in London) dated Aberdeen May 5th 1791. Extract: "I hope you will excuse the trouble I am going to give you. It will be doing me a very particular favour, if you would send for Mr. Hunter the surgeon and give him the enclosed letter from me, it is about getting a proper shoe for George's foot, as I cannot get a right one made here. Mr. Hunter some time ago wrote to Dr. Livingstone, giving him directions how it should be made, but it never was right (sic) made or it would have answered better, and as Mr. Hunter saw George when he was born, I am in hopes, he will be able to give directions for a proper shoe to be made, without seeing it (sic) again. Nothing but want of money prevents my sending him up to London for Mr. Hunter to see his foot."

2*

same period (*summer of 1806*) — were the then romance of the most romantic period of my life".[1]

There are many reasons against considering the person who inspired this 'pure love and passion' as the girl in boy's clothing, who was domesticated with Byron at Brompton in 1808, who, at least on one occasion, was introduced by him to acquaintances as his brother Gordon, and whose reply to the remark of a lady at Brighton concerning the beauty of her (the girl's) horse, was, "Yes it was *gave* me by my brother."[2] There is, as yet, no published evidence that Byron knew this girl previous to 1808. That she could scarcely have been anything but a 'sancy *fille de joie*' as Jeaffreson[3] terms her, is sufficiently proved, by the fact of her having followed around in male attire, a highly egotistical youth of eighteen. This girl has been considered as the original of 'Thyrza' by Minto, the author of several short articles on Byron,[4] but to make this appear highly improbable, it is sufficient to quote the eight and ninth stanzas of the poem 'To Thyrza', written on the 11th of October 1811.[5]

> "Ours too the glance none saw besides;
> The smile none else might understand;
> The whispered thoughts of hearts allied,
> The pressure of the thrilling hand."

> "The kiss so guiltless and refined
> That love each warmer wish forbore;

---

[1] 'Life, Letters, and Journals of Lord Byron' by Thomas Moore. 1 vol. edition, London, 1838, p. 32. (23.)

[2] 'More's Life' etc. 1 vol. ed. p. 70.

[3] 'The Real Lord Byron, the Story of the Poet's Life. Standard ed. p. 120.

[4] See article on Byron in the 9th edition of the 'Encyclopedia Brittanica', — also the Athenaeum for 1876, II, p. 306.

[5] Elze is of the opinion that Thyrza died in Oct. 1811. See the 3rd edition of his work p. 123.

> Those eyes proclaimed so pure a mind
> Even passion blushed to plead for more."

In his letter to Dallas written on the same day that he composed the above verses, Byron writes, — "I have been again shocked with a *death*, and have lost one very dear to me in happier times; but 'I have almost forgot the taste of grief', and 'supped full of horrors' till I have become callous, nor have I a tear left for an event which, *five years ago*, would have bowed down my head to the earth."[1] "Five years ago' would have been in 1806, when under the influence of the 'pure love and passion'. Dallas replies, — "I thank you for your confidential communication at the bottom of the stanza (*stanza 9, canto 2, of 'Childe Harold' — This stanza does not refer to Eddlestone[2] as the note in Murrays 1864 ed. of Byron's works has it.*) which so much delighted me. How truly do I wish that the being to whom that verse now belongs had lived, and lived yours! What your obligations to her would have been in that case is inconceivable."[3] Dallas who was related to the Byron family by marriage, was not the man to recommend the girl in boy's clothing to the chief of the house as a suitable spouse. Moreover 'Thyrza' was dead before Byron's return to England in July 1811, but he was not aware of the fact till the 11th of the following October,

> "And oft I thought at Cynthia's noon,
> When sailing o'er the Ægean wave,
> "Now Thyrza gazes on that moon"—
> Alas, it gleamed upon her grave!"

whereas the girl in boy's clothing was alive and seen

---

[1] 'Moore's Life' etc., letter 71.

[2] Tozer in his edition of Childe Harold makes the same mistake. — 'Childe Harold' edited with introduction and notes by H. F. Tozer. M. A., second edition, Oxford, 1888. See Dallas, 'Recollections of the Life of Lord Byron'. London, 1824, p. 148.

[3] R. C. Dallas, 'Recollections of the Life of Lord Byron'. London, 1824, p. 147.

by Dallas in 1812, after the publication of the first two cantos of 'Childe Harold'.[1]

That Thyrza was not Eddlestone, as the author of an article written for the 'Athenæum' of July 5th 1884 surmised is self-evident. Why should Byron have written of her as of a female to Dallas and in his poems, had the individual in his mind been a male? Jeaffreson's supposition, the hint of which he probably got from Trelawny,[2] who knew nothing about the matter, that Margaret Parker, the poet's cousin, who died a year or two after Byron saw her for the last time in 1800, and to whose memory the feeble elegy in the 'Hours of Idleness' was written in 1802, was "the chief, if not the only inspiring force of the 'Poems to Thyrza',"[3] is certainly, as Bleibtreu[4] maintains, absurd to anyone who has read the poems in question. Bleibtreu[5] follows Minto's example and believes 'Thyrza and the girl in page's clothing to be identical.[6]

Who 'Thyrza' was, is not, and will probably never be known, unless the publication of the Hobhouse papers, those of Hobhouse's eldest daughter Lady Dorchester, or Byron's letters from Italy, which were seen by the author of the

[1] Dallas' 'Recollections' pp. 147, 48.

[2] Trelawny's 'Recollections' of the Last Days of Shelley and Byron'. London. 1858, p. 197.

[3] The Real Lord Byron, standard ed. p 75.

[4] Geschichte der Englischen Litteratur im Neunzehnten Jahrhundert von Karl Bleibtreu, 2te Auflage, p. 232 and fol.

[5] Geschichte der Englischen Litteratur im Neunzehnten Jahrhundert p. 244.

[6] Nanny Smith an old servant of Newstead Abbey said to Washington Irving as regards the boy in girl's clothing: "Once, it is true he had a beautiful boy as a page, which the house-maids said was a girl. * * *. The house-maids however, were very jealous, one of them in particular took the matter in great dudgeon. Her name was Lucy, she was a great favourite with Lord Byron; and had been much noticed by him, and began to have high notions" See Washington Irving's Abbotsford and Newstead Abbey, London 1850. p. 77.

articles in the 'Quarterly Review' in 1869 and 1870, [1] clear up the matter. The only existing clue to the identity of 'Thyrza' to be found in the materials for investigation, which, up to the present date, are at the disposal of a student of Byron's life, is, that 'Thyrza' probably inspired the 'pure love and passion' in 1806. That she was neither Eddlestone, Margaret Parker, nor the girl in boy's clothing, it seems unnecessary to repeat.

II.

On the Probability of Byron's having had an illegitimate Child before the *Birth* of *'Allegra'*.

If the stanzas 'To my Son' [2] and the date affixed [1870] be founded on fact, which their simple and heartfelt character,

---

[1] 'Quarterly Review' for January 1870, p. 228 Extract.—"From his (*Byron's*) leaving England till his death, the sister was the recognised medium of communication between him and his wife; and all his letters to his sister, no matter what their character, appear to have been regularly submitted to Lady Byron, who took copies of them. It does not appear that this was done with his knowledge. He wrote not less than twice a month on an average; and, with passing intervals of irritation and despondency rattled on in much the same manner as in his published letters to his friends. He mentions in more guarded language, his principal liasons, especially that which gave birth to 'Allegra', and the first which seriously occupied him at Venice; and his account of his first meeting with the Countess Guiccioli is as glowing as if it was written for an unconcerned reader. The general tone towards Lady Byron is kind and even affectionate. It is only when the galling consequences of the separation, his exile and shirred name come back upon him that he breaks out."

[2] Murray's 1 vol. ed. of Byron's poetical works. London, 1864, p. 537. Byron writes to Moore on January 5th 1816 ('Moores' Life' etc., letter 232): "I would gladly—or, rather, sorrowfully comply with your request of a dirge for the poor girl you mention. But how can I write on one I have never seen or known? . . . . . I could not write upon any thing, without some personal experience and foundation.

besides a passage in the 12th and one in the 16th canto of 'Don Juan',[1]

> "There was a country girl in a close cap
> And scarlet cloak (I hate the sight to see, since—
> Since—since—in youth, I had the sad mishap—
> But luckily I have paid few parish fees since):
> That scarlet cloak, alas! alas unclosed with rigour,
> Presents the problem of a double figure."

> "A reel within a bottle is a mystery,
> One can't tell how it e'er got in or out;
> Therefore the present piece of natural history
> I leave to those who are fond of solving doubt;
> And merely state, though not for the consistory
> Lord Henry was a justice, and that Scout
> The constable beneath a warrant's banner
> Had bagged this poacher upon Nature's manor."

several passages in the poet's letters to his mother,[2] and two passages in letters written to Moore[3] seem to vouchsafe, Byron was a father in his twentieth year. some months, possibly not a year, after the first glow of his passion for 'Thyrza'.[4] He writes to Moore from Venice on February 2nd 1818. "I know how to feel with you, because (selfishness being always the substratum of our damnable clay) I am quite wrapt up in my own children. Besides my little legitimate, I have made unto myself an *il*legimate since (to say nothing of one before)."[5]

Now either the poem 'To my Son' must be altogether fictitious, or Medora Leigh cannot have been Lord Byron's child, or Byron must have written Moore that he had had one illegitimate child before the birth of 'Allegra', whereas

---

[1] Canto 16, stanzas 61, 62,—see also canto 12, stanzas 17, 18.

[2] 'Moore's Life' etc., letters 45. 52.

[3] 'Moore's Life' etc, letters 137, 307.

[4] The mother of this child he calls Helen, and writes of her as dead in 1807. See verses 'To my Son'.

[5] 'Moore's Life' etc., letter 307.

in fact, he had had two,—a very unlikely thing for a man of Byron's temperament to do, who from his fondness for describing himself as romantically naughty, would have been more inclined to increase than diminish the number. It will appear to those who consider what Charles Mackay wrote in the preface to his book on Medora Leigh,[1] after carefully studying the documents in his possession (that she, Medora Leigh, 'was the undoubted daughter of Lord Byron's sister') and who knows the utter absurdity of the Beecher Stowe scandal, that this girl, whoever she may have been, was no child of Lord Byron, although Bleibtreu[2] considers it certain that she was.

Bleibtreu[3] gives as one of his reasons for considering Medora Leigh as a child of Byron, the peculiarity of her name. What could be more natural for Mrs. Leigh, than to christen her child 'Medora', after the beloved of the 'Corsair' of the same name, out of honour to her brother, whose poem 'The Corsair', which had so prodigious a success, was published in the beginning of 1815? Medora Leigh, according to her own statement, was born in 1814.[4] That Lady Byron told this unfortunate girl in 1840 at Fontainebleau, that Lord Byron had been her father,[5] cannot by any means be taken as fact without any further evidence, when one considers how Lady Byron hated Mrs. Leigh ever since they quarreled in 1829, and with what utter disregard for truth she slandered her dead husband's half-sister in her latter days.

Two passages in Byron's unpublished letters to his half-sister, written just before leaving England in 1816, show

---

[1] 'Medora Leigh: A History and an Autobiography'. London 1869, p. 6.

[2] Bleibtreu: 'Geschichte der Englischen Litteratur im Neunzehnten Jahrhundert', 2nd ed. p. 227.

[3] Geschichte der Englischen Litteratur im 19ten Jahrhundert, 2nd ed. p. 245.

[4] 'Medora Leigh', p. 91.

[5] 'Medora Leigh', pp. 135, 36.

that he possessed a strong interest in Medora Leigh. He writes Mrs. Leigh on the 15th of April 1816,—"Tell me how is Georgey and *Do [abbreviation for Medora]*,—and on April 22nd 1816, three days before leaving England,—"Of the child you will inform me and write about poor dear little *Do*."[1]

Mrs. Leigh wrote to Hodgson on March 18th 1815[2] (3) — "If I may give you mine [*opinion*] it is, that in his [*Byron's*] own mind, there were and are recollections fatal to his peace, and which would have prevented his being happy with any woman whose excellence equalled or approached that of Lady B., from the consciousness of being unworthy of it."

What these 'recollections fatal to his peace' were, is known, if known at all, to but few individuals. At any rate, Bleibtreu, according to Mrs. Leigh's testimony, was probably correct in stating that Byron had substantial reasons for his melancholy, and for writing the self-accusatory passages in Manfred, which made Goethe think that Byron had committed a murder.[3]

One of these passages,

"Man. I loved her and destroyed her!
Witch. With thy hand?
Man. Not with my hand but heart—which broke her heart—
It gazed on mine and withered. I have shed
Blood, but not hers—and yet her blood was shed—
I saw—and could not staunch it"

Makes one involuntarily recall the fate which the second Mrs. Shelley so nearly underwent on the 16th of June 1822

---

[1] Add. MS. 31 037 pp. 35,37 British Museum.
[2] Probably falsely dated 1815 instead of 1816. 'Athenaeum' September 19th 1885.
[3] Bleibtreu: 'Englische Litteraturgeschichte im 19. Jahrhundert.' 2nd ed. p. 191.

at San Terenzo.[1] This passage to judge from that immediately preceeding,

> "Man. She was like me in lineaments—her eyes
> Her hair, her features, all, to the very tone
> Even of her voice, they said were like to mine."

Probably refers to 'brother Gordon' the 'girl in boy's clothing', whose face so much ressembled Byron's, as Minto first suggested in the Athenæum in 1876,[2] and whose sudden disappearance from the field of Byronic biography after Dallas[3] saw her in the spring of 1812, is such a mystery.

III.

Some Remarks on the Article in 'The Edinburgh Review' on 'Hours of Idleness'.

That the 'Edinburgh Review' article on 'Hours of Idleness' was not published in January 1808, as Jeaffreson has it,[4] is evident from Byron's letter to Beecher,[5] dated February 26th 1808, in which he writes, — "I am of so much importance that a most violent attack is preparing for me in the next number of the 'Edinburgh Review'. This I had from the authority of a friend who has seen the proof and manuscript of the critique."

The general opinion is that Brougham wrote the article. James Henry Dixon in 'Notes and Queries' for December 8th 1870, writes,—"It is beyond all dispute that the Late Lord Brougham did write the famous article in 'The Edinburgh Review',"—he also mentions a Paris edition of Byron's works edited by Galt, in which a dictum of Brougham's is

---

[1] Dowden's 'Life of Shelley' vol 2, p. 514,—or Jeaffreson's 'The Real Shelley' vol 2, p. 439.

[2] 'Athenæum' 1876, II, p. 306.

[3] Dallas' 'Recollections' pp. 243, 49.

[4] 'The Real Lord Byron' standard ed. p. 97.

[5] 'Moore's Life' etc, letter 24.

quoted to the effect, that there 'was not one word in that review of which he (Brougham) was ashamed.' 'Notes and Queries' for October 29th 1870, quotes 'The Mirror' of July 2th 1830, as follows: 'It may not be generally known that the present Lord Chancellor Brougham is the real author of the famous article in 'The Edinburgh Review' on Byron's juvenile production, 'Hours of Idleness'... We have this fact from authority on which we can place the utmost reliance.' Rogers[1] quotes Byron as having said in Italy, "on being at last assured that the celebrated critique on his early poems in 'The Edinburgh Review' was by Lord Brougham, —'If ever I return to England Brougham shall hear from me'."[2]

That the 'impulse of the blow' came from Cambridge, as Jeaffreson keenly observes,[3] seems highly probable. What besides anger caused by the impertinent and ungentlemanly satire in 'Hours of Idleness' on the officials of the Cambridge university, could have occasioned such severity on the part of the reviewer. Had Brougham, who, since 1804, was resident in London, been a witness of Byron's wild life in town in the early months of 1808; or had Brougham an intimate friend, or friends, amongst the Cambridge university officials of that time? Or was the boyish egotism in some of the poems and in the preface to 'Hours of Idleness', alone responsible for the severity of the article?[1]

---

[1] 'The Table Talk of Samuel Rogers.' London 1856, p. 234.

[2] See also the Countess Guiccioli's work 'Lord Byron jugé par les Temoins de sa vie.' Paris, 1869, vol I, p. 84.

[3] 'The Real Lord Byron', standard ed. p. 100.

[4] According to Trelawny, Byron said to him on board 'The Hercules', that he, Byron, had 'reduced his hates to two, that venomous reptile Brougham and Southey the apostate'. Trelawny's 'Records of Shelley, Byron and the Author'. London 1887, p. 205.

IV.

Diverse minor points.

That Byron had other reasons than the annoyance caused him by creditors, for leaving England with Hobhouse in the early summer of 1809, he himself definately states in a letter to his sollicitor Hanson. In this letter written at Newstead Abbey, and dated April 16, 1809, he writes,—"If the consequences of my leaving England were ten times as ruinous as you describe, I have no alternative, there are circumstances which render it absolutely indispensable, and quit the country I must immediately".[1]

Galt[2] attributed Byron's frequent scowling at Gibraltar to recollections of some 'unpleasant reminiscence', and describes the young man's behavior on board the Mediterranean packet, as 'suggesting dim reminiscences of him who shot the albatros,' in Coleridge's poem 'The Ancient Mariner'. Hobhouse, his travelling companion at that time, said to Moore on the 28th of April 1822, some five months before he visited Byron for the last time. "I know more of Byron than anyone else, and much more than I should wish anybody else to know".[3] This remark of Hobhouse, one might think with propriety to refer to this period of his friend's career. There were others who saw more of the poet, from the summer of 1811 when he returned from Greece till he left his native country for good, in the spring of 1816. That Hobhouse was in complete ignorance of many of the most important incidents of Byron's life in Italy, is amply proved by that portion of his article in the 'Westminster Review' which

---

[1] Egerton MS. 2611, p. 113, British Museum.

[2] Galt's 'Life of Byron'. London. 1830, p. 63.

[3] 'Memoirs, Correspondence and Journal of Thomas Moore' edited by Lord John Russell. London. 1853. vol 3. p. 347.

treats of Medwin's book.[1] Of course in his remark to Moore, Hobhouse may have referred to his friends life as a whole, but there was no period of it with which he was more familiar than from the fall of 1807, when he and Byron first became friends, till they parted in the summer of 1810.

Jeaffreson writes as regards 'The Giaour',—"It is still to be shown that the poem was based on one of the poet's adventures in Greece."[2] Hobhouse, the author of the article on Medwin and Dallas in the 'Westminster Review' for January 1825,[3] writes,—"The girl whose life Lord Byron saved at Athens, was not an object of his lordship's attachment—but that of his lordship's Turkish servant."[4] Byron corresponded with Hobhouse from Greece after his friend left him for England, and was also no doubt abundantly communicative to the companion of the first year of his travels with regard to the experiences of his second year abroad, after his return to England. That Byron wrote Hobhouse about one of the incidents which afterwards gave rise to 'The Corsair', may be ascertained by consulting Hobhouses letter of April 23rd 1811 to Hanson, from Dover.[5],[6]

---

[1] 'Journal of the Conversations of Lord Byron at Pisa'; by Thomas Medwin. London, 1824.

[2] 'The Real Lord Byron', standard ed. p. 170.

[3] For proof of Hobhouse having been the author of this article, see his letters to Mrs. Leigh. Add. MS. 31 037, British Museum.

[4] 'Westminster Review' for January 1825.

[5] Egerton MS. 2611, p. 231, British Museum.

[6] Trelawny makes Byron say: 'There is a rocky islet off Maina— it is the pirates Isle; it suggested the "Corsair". No one knows it Ill show you the spot on the way to the Morea. There is the spot I should like my bones to be.' See Trelawny's Records 3rd ed. 1887.

V.

Some new Views regarding the Separation of Lord and Lady Byron.

For those who would understand what, under certain aspects, was the character of the young man whose hand Miss Miibanke accepted in the autumn of 1814, and married in the following January; it is necessary, at least, to glance rapidly over the sort of preliminary schooling for conjugal felicity, which Byron underwent from shortly after the publication of the first two cantos of 'Childe Harold' till he made his second proposal to his future wife in September 1814, and to consider how those 'dispositions' were developed, which Lady Byron, after determining never again to live under the same roof with her husband in January 1816, considered as so 'anti-domestic' that she 'hoped to be remembered' by him 'only as a burden'.[1]

It is a well known fact that the English 'higher classes' of the early years of the present century were exceedingly profligate—profligate to an extent not to be readily conceived by the English of to day, and that Byron was certainly one of the most reckless libertines of his time, till he sobered down to an orderly and quiet life after his Venetian excesses.

Before coming of age, Byron had been thoroughly initiated into various kinds of dissipation at Cambridge, and though he may have been putting it rather strong when he wrote to Dallas in January 1808,—"I have been held up as the votary of licentiousness and the disciple of infidelity,"[2] yet there are no sufficient reasons for thinking as Moore did,

---

[1] See Lady Byron's letter of January 25th 1816 to Mrs. Leigh,— No. 13 in the appendix to the standard edition of 'The Real Lord Byron',—also to be found in 'The Athenaeum' for August 18th 1883.

[2] 'Moore's Life etc.', letter 20.

that his letters to Miss Pigot make a 'display and boast of rakishness',[1] and that the young peer did not intend them as unvarnished chronicles of his doings.

From the day of his arrival in England from Greece in July 1811, till the first two cantos of 'Childe Harold' were published on February 29th 1812, Byron was sufficiently busy to be out of mischief with revising his poetry, composing new stanzas, transacting business with Hanson and composing his maiden speech for the House of Lords; but hardly two months had passed since the two cantos appeared, than the long list of his scrapes with women and dissipations recommences.[2]

On August 22nd 1813 about one year and four months after this first scrape as recorded in his short letters of this period to Moore, he writes to the same correspondent, — "I am in a far more serious, and entirely new scrape than any of the last twelve months, — and that is saying a good deal. It is unlucky we can neither live with or without these women."[3] In his journal for November 17th of the same year, he writes, — "Not a word from * * Have they set out from *.*? or has my last precious epistle fallen into the lion's jaws? If so — and this silence looks suspicious — I must clap on my 'musty morion' and 'hold out my iron' — I am out of practice — but I won't begin again at Manton's now. Besides, I would not return his shot. I was once a famous wafer-splitter; but then the bullies of society made it necessary. Ever since I began to feel I had a bad cause to support, I have left off the exercise."[4] On April 9th 1814 he writes to Moore, — that he has been "breaking a few of the favourite commandments" but that he means to pull „up and marry" if anyone will have him.[5]

---

[1] 'Moore's Life' etc., note to letter 18.
[2] 'Moore's Life' etc., p. 164.
[3] 'Moore's Life' etc., letter 133.
[4] 'Moore's Life' etc., p. 201 (one volume ed.).
[5] 'Moore's Life' etc., letter 173.

On the 15th of the following September the letter containing his second proposal to Miss Milbanke was on its way to the lady, on the 2nd, of January 1815 they were married, and but little more than a year had passed since their engagement, than she had probably strong reasons for suspecting him of infidelity.

Moore writes, — "It is, at the same time, very far from my intention to allege that, in the course of the noble poet's intercourse with the theatre, he was not sometimes led into a line of acquaintance and converse unbefitting, if not dangerous to, the steadiness of married life. But the imputations against him on this head were (as far as affected, his conjugal character) not the less unfounded, — as the sole case in which he afforded anything like *real* grounds for an accusation did not take place till *after* the period of the separation." [1]

Moore was probably relying on the information he obtained from Byron's memoirs in making this assertion, but it is doubtful if Byron positively knew of his wife's chief reasons for repudiating him. Lady Byron persistently refused to inform him of her principal grounds for action, with which only the counsellors on both sides. Dr. Lushington and Sir Samuel Romilly, Mrs. Leigh, and the other individual named in the 'Quarterly Review' for January 1870 were acquainted; and had sworn complete secrecy as regards her chief motives for action to some interested person or persons, unless the case should go into court. [2]

---

[1] 'Moore's Life' etc., p. 297 (one volume ed.).

[2] See her statements in Campbell's article on Moore's Life of Byron in 'The New Monthly' 1830, I, p. 379. Extract: "It is not true that pecuniary embarrassments were the cause of the disturbed state of Lord Byron's mind, or formed the chief reason for the arrangements made by him at that time (*to go abroad?*). But is it reasonable for me to expect that you, or anyone else, should believe this, unless I show what were the causes in question? and this I cannot do."

I am, &c. &c.

E. (*sic*) Noel Byron.

3

In the British Museum are preserved in one of the open collections of Byronic writings, some verses in the handwriting of Lady Byron entitled 'The Magpie',[1] and bearing the postmark September 28th 1815,[2] in which the so-called committee of 'mismanagement of Drury Lane Theatre is ridiculed as a whole, after which Byron comes in for his share as a member:

"Then there's Byron ashamed to appear like a Poet,
He talkes of finances for fear he should show it —
And makes all the envious Dandys despair;
By the cut of his shirt, and the curl of his hair?"

Under these verses Lady Byron wrote her husband's half-sister, — "I have not got the others down get — I believe B — will go to the Theatre to night but you seem to have mistaken!—for the mischief has not lately taken place *there* but *after* his return — when alone — I grow more unable to sit up late."[3]

In Byron's last letter to his wife before leaving England,[4] he writes, — that when he made the will in favour of Mrs. Leigh and her children *(July 29th 1815)* he and his wife "had not then differed." In Lady Byron's letter of February 23rd 1816,[5] to her husband, she wrote that she had "warned him," before thinking him mad, "earnestly and affectionately of the irreparable consequenses which must issue" from his conduct both to himself and her — and that "to those representations" he had replied "by a determination to be wicked" though it should break her heart. She continues, — "I cannot attribute your 'State of mind' to any

[1] See Byron's letter of September 25th 1815 to Murray as regards this poem ('Moore's Life' etc., one volume ed. p. 285).
[2] Add. MS. 31037, p. 21, British Museum.
[3] Add. MS. 31037, p. 21, British Museum.
[4] Letter No. 19 in the appendix to the standard edition of 'The Real Lord Byron'; also in the 'Athenæum' for August 18th 1883.
[5] Letter No. 18 of the appendix to the standard edition of 'The Real Lord Byron';—also in the Athenæum' for August 18th 1883.

cause so much as to the total dereliction of principle, which *since* our marriage you have professed and gloried in" On what subject besides respect for marriage vows did Byron lack principle? Was he not an honest man according to the 'code of honour' of the world of fashion of his day? And yet Jeaffreson writes in his work on Byron. which, on most points is teeming with sagacity and penetration, that — "It is certain that Lady Byron and her husband separated on account of reasons covered by the familiar and elastic phrase 'incompatibility of temper'." [1] Why is it certain? Because Lady Lovelace thought so? Unless Jeaffreson can publish documents to verify his assertion, it is of course impossible to accept it as true in the face of so much published evidence to the contrary.

VI.

Byron's Relationship to Mary Jane Clairmont.

Whether Mary Jane Clairmont, [2] daughter of William Godwin's second wife by a former husband and mother of Byron's natural child 'Allegra'. was the cause of the poet's being led astray from the path of conjugal duty as early as the lines written by his wife under the verses entitled 'The Magpie' suggest, I am unable to decide, not having been able to obtain sufficient information on the subject for any positive conclusion. The substance of the lines written by Lady Byron to Mrs. Leigh, agrees with the account which a gentleman of literary eminence in London (*who claims to*

---

[1] 'The Real Lord Byron', standard edition, p. 188.

[2] Generally called 'Claire' by Shelleyan and Byronic biographers. she was called 'Claire' by Shelley, by her sister-by-affinity Mary Godwin (afterwards the second Mrs. Shelley), Leigh Hunt, Mrs. Hunt, and other from the spring of 1814 on. By her mother, brother, father-in-law and Fanny Imlay she was invariably called 'Jane'.

3*

to have had the story from an intimate friend of Byron, who had obtained his information from the poet] gave me of the manner in which Byron first became intimate with Miss Clairmont. The second Mrs. Shelley however writes to 'Claire' herself of the 'spring when she [*Claire*] became acquainted with Lord Byron;[1] and Medwin, Shelley's cousin, who might well have obtained some information on the subject from Shelley or Shelley's second wife, writes,—"She was not altogether a stranger to Byron when they met at Sécheron; for as he was about to quit London for the continent in the spring of that year [*1816*], after his mysterious repudiation by Lady Byron, she had an interview with him for the purpose of obtaining an engagement at Drury Lane .....; but which object, his recent resignation of office as chairman of the committee of management, precluded him as he explained to her from forwarding."[2]

Mrs. Marshall, in her well known work on Shelley's second wife, writes—"Nothing in Clara's [*Claire's*] letters to him (Byron) (which unfortunately may not be published) goes to prove that she was very deeply in love with him."[3] That Claire was far from having an affectionate remembrance of Byron after his death, may be seen from one of her letters to Mrs. Shelley, in which, in referring to the latter's novel 'Lodore' (*published in 1835*) she writes,—"Mrs.—admired '*Lodore*' amazingly, so do I, or should I, if it were not for that modification of the beastly character of Lord Byron of which you have composed Lodore, * * * Good God! to think a person of your genius, whose moral tact ought to be proportionately exalted, should think it a task befitting its powers, to gild and embellish and pass off as beautiful what was the merest compound of vanity, folly, and every miserable weakness that ever met together in one human being! As I do not want to be severe

---

[1] Dowden's 'Life of Shelley'. vol. 2, p. 489.
[2] Medwin's Life of Shelley. vol. 1, p. 280 (London 1847).
[3] 'The Life and Letters of Mary Wollstonecraft Shelley' by Mrs. Julian Marshall. London, 1889, vol. 1, p. 125.

on the poor man, because he is dead and cannot defend himself. I have only taken the lighter defects of his character, or else I might say that never was a nature more profoundly corrupt than his became, or more radically vulgar than his was from the very outset. Never was there an individual less adapted, except perhaps Alcibiades, for being held up as anything but an object of commiseration, or as an example of how contemptible is even intellectual greatness when not joined with moral greatness."[1]

Byron certainly cared very little for this girl, whose behaviour, to say the least, must have been very irritating to a man of his temperament. With what outbursts of passion she assailed him at Geneva, we are not informed, but to judge from the few of her letters to him which have been published,[2] and which are by no means as restrained as good policy required, she must have overwhelmed him with sarcasm when in anger in his presence. Possibly also the similarity of her name to that of the 'mischief maker' Mrs. Clermont,[3] whom Byron considered in February 1816, as "very much the occult cause of his domestic discrepancies,"[4] and whom he poured his wrath upon in the verses called 'A Sketch', influenced him to some degree in disliking Claire.[5]

---

[1] 'The Life and Letters of Mary Wollstonecraft Shelley'. vol. 2, pp. 265, 66.

[2] Besides many of Claire's letters to Byron, those which Shelley wrote him announcing the birth of Allegra and others in behalf of the child and mother, and Byron's letters in reply, if he wrote any, have as yet not been published.

[3] Mary Shelley spelt this woman's name 'Claremont', see her letter to Trelawny, vol. 2, pp. 118, 19, 20; of Mrs. Marshall's work.

[4] 'Moore's Life' etc., letter 233.

[5] Jeaffreson confounds Mrs. Clermont the 'Mischief-maker' and former governess of Lady Byron whom he attacked in his poem called 'The Sketch' with Mrs. Clairmont Godwin's second wife and mother of Claire. He writes: "Several motives are conceivable, any, one of which would dispose the 'Mischief-maker' to find her former pupil to withhold the informations from her father and mother. Care for Jane's welfare and

Almost five years after Byron saw the last of her in August 1816 at Geneva, she wrote him on the 24th of March 1821 from Florence,—"How will Lady Byron, never yet justified for her conduct towards you be soothed and rejoice in the honourable safety of herself and child, and all the world be bolder to praise her prudence, my unhappy Allegra furnishing the (damning — *left clearly legible*) condemning evidence." [1]

It is not necessary to possess much knowledge of Byron's sensitiveness to all hostile criticism of his conduct, to picture to oneself, into what a fury this passage in Claire's letter must have set him. That he had no doubt received many a sharp cut from 'Claire's' tongue previous to receiving this letter, one may reasonably conjecture from his having expressed to Hoppner, as Shelley wrote to his second wife from Venice in August 1818, 'his extreme horror of her *[Claire's]* arrival, and the necessity which it would impose on him of instantly quitting Venice.' [2]

Shelley described Claire's character, after Allegra's death in a letter to John Gisborne thus: "C—*[Claire]* is with us, and the death of her child seems to have restored her to

dread of her displeasure, concern for Jane's reputation and concern for her own advantage, May have made Mrs. Clermont urgent with Lady Byron to keep from every one but her lawyers a matter so discreditable to the girl and her connections. The Mischief-makers natural preference for secrecy may have been stimulated by regard for Godwin's feelings." (Real Lord Byron, standard ed. p. 208.) *Mrs. Clermont* the 'Mischief-maker', had nothing to do with either Godwin's second wife *Mrs. Clairmont* or with either Godwin or Claire. This is probably the single mistake Jeaffreson writes of having discovered in his work on Byron in the preface to his edition of 1884. If so, why did he not correct it?

[1] Egerton MS. 2332 B., British Museum.

[2] Dowden's 'Life of Shelley' vol. 2, p. 226.—Shelley in one of his letters from Ravenna to his wife, dated Aug. 10th 1821, wrote her in referring probably to Claire and Byron,—"He *[Byron]* would like Pisa were it not for * * * *[Claire]*. Gunpowder and fire ought to be kept at a respectable distance from each other". (H. Buxton Forman's edition of 'Shelley's Prose Works'. vol. 4, p. 217.)

tranquillity. Her character is somewhat altered. She is vivacious and talkative; and though she teases me sometimes, I like her."[1]

Byron agreed to take care of their child, Allegra, in the spring of 1818, on the 'sole condition' that, from the day it left her, the mother entirely relinquished it, and never saw it again.'[2] A few months later, when requested by *Claire* through Shelley for permission to see her child: he said according to Shelley.—'Why Claire will be as unwilling to part with her again as she is to be absent from her now, and there will be a second renewal of affliction and a second parting. But if you like, she shall go to Claire to Padua for a week; and in fact, after all, I have no right over the child. If Claire likes to take it, let her take it. I do not say what most people would in that situation, that I will refuse to provide for it, or abandon it, if she does this; but she must surely be aware herself how very imprudent such a measure would be."[3]

Mrs. Shelley who went to see Byron's remains in Great George Street, Westminster, questioned Byron's valet Fletcher about the poet's death, and wrote to Trelawny on July 28th 1824, that—"from a few words, which he *[Fletcher]* had imprudently let fall. it would seem that his Lord spoke of Claire in his last moments, and of his wish to do something for her, at a time when his mind, vacillating between consciousness and delirium, would not permit him to do anything."[1]

[1] 'P. B. Shelley's Prose Works', edited by Harry Buxton Forman. London, 1880. vol. 4, p. 279.

[2] 'The Life and Letters of Mary Wollstonecraft Shelley'. vol. 1. p. 212.

[3] Dowden's 'Life of Shelley' vol. 2, p. 226.

[1] 'The Life and Letters of Mary Wollstonecraft Shelley'. vol. 2 pp. 118, 19, 20.

VII.

Preliminary Arrangements for the Meeting of Shelley, Mary Godwin, Mary Jane Clairmont and Lord Byron, at Dejean's Hôtel d'Angleterre at Sécheron (near Geneva).

Those writers on Shelley who have used the 'Shelley papers', have up to the present day, with but one exception. persisted in representing the meeting of Shelley. Claire, Mary Godwin and Byron at Dejean's Hôtel d'Angleterre at Sécheron as accidental, or that Claire persuaded Shelley and Mary Godwin to go to Geneva with her, without informing them of her *liason* with Byron.

Jeaffreson in 'The Real Lord Byron', wrote with reason, that the circumstantial evidence, against this having been the case, is 'overwhelming'.[1]

It was not however till 1889, that Mrs. Julian Marshall in her work on Shelley's second wife, writing with the 'Shelley papers' at her disposal, confessed that Shelley had entertained the 'prospect of a possible companionship' with Byron, before leaving England in the spring of 1816.[2]

Dowden, obtaining his information from an undated letter of Miss Clairmont to Byron, maintains that on leaving England with Shelley, Mary Godwin "did not so much as know that Byron was acquainted with Miss Clairmont's name,"[3] — and in his introduction to his edition of Shelley's 'Poetic Works', goes so far as to write that not only Mary Godwin but also Shelley "were in profound ignorance of Byron's intrigue with Miss Clairmont, when they started from England."[4]

---

[1] 'The Real Lord Byron' standard ed p. 237.

[2] 'The Life and Letters of Mary Wollstonecraft Shelley' by Mrs. Julian Marshall. London, 1889. vol. 1. pp. 128, 29.

[3] Dowden's 'Life of Shelley' vol. 2, p. 6.

[4] Dowden's edition of Shelley's 'Poetic Works'. London, 1890, Introduction p. 23.

If Prof. Dowden has conclusive documentary proof to back up this most remarkable statement, nothing but the publication of the same could possibly make thinking people believe that Shelley required his mistress to journey in those non railway days, with her infant boy, a little over three months old,[1] and Claire, (a companion that this lady, who was destined to become the second Mrs. Shelley, was so anxious to get rid of in the spring of the previous year[2] to Geneva, without telling her the 'why and the wherefore' of such most extraordinary doings. That Shelley however knew of Claire's intimacy with Byron is indisputable. Shelley was not the man to be foolish enough to think that Claire, of whose "incapacity for the slightest degree of friendship" (*that is she wanted something more*[3] he wrote in his journal for October 14th 1814, had fallen into a trance of platonic affection for Byron, the most celebrated rake of his day; neither was Shelley silly enough to think that Byron, whose reputation on such matters was far from good, had fallen into a sort of spiritual admiration for the girl, whom he, Shelley, had converted to his own ideas of 'free love'.[4]

According to Mrs. Marshall, Mary Godwin was probably introduced to Byron in March 1816, "when Shelley and Mary were, for a short time staying up in town."[5] It does not seem at all probable, that if Mary Godwin was able to obtain an introduction to Byron, that Shelley who was living openly and confessedly with her in terms of conjugal intimacy, and had the *entrée* into all houses and all societies where

---

[1] Shelley's second child by Mary Godwin, born January 24th 1816.

[2] See Dowden's 'Life of Shelley' vol. 1, p. 518. Mary Godwin wrote to her future husband two months after returning from Geneva,—"Give me a garden and *absentia* Claire, and I will thank my love for many favours (Dowden's 'Life of Shelley' vol. 2, p. 62).

[3] See index to 'The Real Shelley' also 'The Real Shelley' vol. 2, p. 254 and Dowden's 'Life of Shelley' vol. 1, p. 483.

[4] See 'The Real Shelley' vol. 2, p. 261.

[5] 'The Life and Letters of Mary Wollstonecraft Shelley' vol. 1, p. 125.

she went, did not have the same opportunity of making Byron's acquaintance, of which he was so desirous. Indeed it seems highly probable that the arrangements for meeting at the hotel at Sécheron were made by the three disciples of 'free love' and the celebrated poet by word of month in England.

VIII.

Byron's Affection for Teresa Gamba Guiccioli.

It is impossible at this distant date, to form an altogether accurate conception of Byron's attitude towards the countess Guiccioli and his affection for her. That his love for this girl countess did not possess that gushing and romantic fervour which Moore attributed to it, is certain; but neither is it to be doubted that he retained a warm affection for her to the last.

Shelley, with his knowledge of Claire's inability to retain Byron's affection, had not known the countess many days, when he wrote on the 22nd of October 1821 to John Gisborne. —'La Guiccioli, who awaits him [*Byron*] impatiently, is a very pretty, sentimental, innocent Italian, who has sacrificed an immense fortune for the sake of Lord Byron, and who, if I know anything of my friend, of her, and of human nature, will hereafter have plenty of leisure and opportunity to repent her rashness."[1]

The American painter West wrote Moore of Byron's having said to him in the summer of 1822,—'that he hoped his connection with the Guiccioli would be for ever.'[2]

Medwin in his 'Conversations with Lord Byron at Pisa'[3] writes,—"Lord Byron is certainly very much attached to her without being actually in love,"—and in the same work.

---

[1] Forman's edition of Shelley's 'Prose Works', vol. 4, p. 243.
[2] 'Moore's Life' etc., p. 562.
[3] London, 1824, p. 23.

referring to the day after Shelley's cremation, he writes,— "The next morning he [*Byron*] was perfectly recovered. When I called, I found him sitting in the garden under the shade of some orange trees with the Countess. They are now always together, and he is become quite domestic. He calls her *Piccinina*, and bestows on her all the pretty diminutive epithets that are so sweet in Italian. His kindness and attention to the Guiccioli have been invariable. A three years' constancy proves that he is not altogether so unmanageable by a sensible woman as might be supposed."[1]

The same author in a work called 'The Angler in Wales',[2] writes, after describing Byron's horses,—"The pair he lent the Guiccioli were better to look at than to go. These we met with the fair Ravennese *en route*, and stopped to hold a short parley with the Contessa. When she was gone, he said,—'I loved her for three weeks. What a red-headed[3] thing it is! I am much obliged to Lady Byron because I cannot marry while she lives'."[1] In the same work he describes Byron, just before the poet sailed for

---

[1] 'Journal of Conversations with Lord Byron at Pisa', by Thomas Medwin. London, 1824, p. 259.

[2] London, 1834, vol. 2, p. 182.

[3] This supposed remark of Byron is very probably a forgery, as West the American painter, who painted a portrait of the Contessa at Montenero, in 1822, describes her hair as 'golden' (see Moore's Life etc., one volume et p. 562), as does also Leigh Hunt ('Lord Byron and some of his Contemporaries'. Paris, 1828, vol. I, p. 67). Lady Blessington writes of Byron's having described to her the Guiccioli's hair as 'auburn' ('Conversations of Lord Byron with the Countess of Blessington', second edition p. 96). This lady had probably forgotten what Byron did say to her, and obtained her information from Medwin's 'Conversations' (p. 23) in which work this 'prince of blunderers' Medwin, describes the colour of the same woman's hair as being of the darkest auburn, and twenty—three years later in his 'Life of Shelley' as bright auburn' (vol. 2, pp. 140, 41). Jeaffreson writing from personal experience, having examined her hair, declares it absolutely golden ('The Real Lord Byron' standard ed. p. 285).

[4] 'The Angler in Wales'. London. 1834, vol. 2, p. 182.

Greece, as "very uncomfortable" and tired of the Contessa."[1] Consul-General Hoppner, Byron's friend and confidant at Venice, wrote to the 'Athenæum' for May 22nd 1869,— "Lady H—[*Holland?*] who saw Lord Byron frequently at Genoa, and also Mme. Guiccioli, assured me she was convinced he went to Greece to yet away from her."

According to Lady Blessington's 'Journal of Conversations of Lord Byron',[2] Byron made the remark in Genoa, sometime after the first of April 1823—'Were the Contessa Guiccioli and I married, we should, I am sure, be cited as an example of conjugal happiness,'—and also,

"Oh! what are a thousand living loves
To that which cannot quit the death?"

'How did I feel this when Allegra, my daughter died! While she lived, her existence never seemed necessary to my happiness; but no sooner did I lose her than it appeared to me as if I could not live without her. Even now the recollection is most bitter; but how much more severely would the death of Teresa afflict me with the dreadful consciousness that while I had been soaring into the realms of romance and fancy, I had left her to weep over my coldness or infidelities of imagination. It is a dreadful proof of the weakness of our natures, that we cannot control ourselves sufficiently to form the happiness of those we love, or bear their loss without agony.'

Lady Blessington continues,—"The whole of this conversation made a deep impression on my mind, and the countenance of the speaker full of earnestness and feeling, impressed it still more strongly on my memory."[3]

In passing judgment on Byron's affection for the Countess Guiccioli, it is well to remember, that when he first met

---

[1] 'The Angler in Wales'. vol. 2, p. 198.
[2] Second edition, London, 1850, p. 116.
[3] 'Conversations of Lord Byron with the Countess of Blessington'. second edition pp. 72, 3.

her, in the spring of 1819, Byron was no more the London dandy-poet, still less the romantic and sentimental schoolboy who fell in love with Mary Anne Chaworth; but the author of the first two cantos of Don Juan, a keen reader of human nature with an abundance of worldly wisdom for his years.

That such a man would have been swayed by any sentimental considerations such as Jeaffreson thinks would have ruled his movements, had he been really in love with the Countess, from installing her in his villa at La Mira, namely: because he had lived there with Marianna Segati, the linen-drapers wife etc.,[1] does not seem at all probable. Indeed it seems as if Jeaffreson, who was doubtless justified in attacking Moore's gushing over the fervour of Byron's attachment to the Countess, had gone a little to far in the opposite direction.

After considering how frequently Byron idealized Teresa Guiccioli in poetic works, from the beginning of their *liason* till he finished 'The Island' in February 1823,[2] besides his frequent affectionate remarks to Lady Blessington concerning her[3] during the last few months of his stay in Genoa, just previous to his departure for Greece, it seems as if the only conclusion one is justified in making, is that he loved her as much as his worldly nature, irritable temper, ruined health and shattered nerves permitted of his loving anyone. Had this not been the case, Byron would not have given Col. Stanhope to understand at Missolonghi, that he (Byron) "preferred Italian women to all others."[4]

---

[1] 'The Real Lord Byron' standard ed. p. 298.

[2] See Bleibtreu's excellent analysis of Byron's Works in his 'Geschichte der englischen Litteratur im neunzehnten Jahrhundert', second edition, Leipzig, 1888.

[3] 'Conversations of Lord Byron with the Countess of Blessington', second edition, pp. 67, 68, 69, 72, 73, 91, 115, 116, 117, 196.

[4] See Col. Stanhope's 'Sketch' of Lord Byron, printed in the appendix to the English translation of Elze's Life of Byron. p. 493.

The great poet's life from his entering Cambridge university till he died in Greece, was composed, with but few intervals of comparative calm, of a continued series of excitements; such as he, who was constantly suffering the pangs of hunger in his struggle against his tendency to fatten,[1] could not dispense with, without rendering existence unendurable.

There can be little doubt that this craving after excitement had much to do, in common with the poet's hatred of tyranny, in causing him to join the Italian Carbonari, and afterwards to aid the Greeks in their struggle for independence. Besides it rendered him unfit for enjoying the quiet of the all but idyllic life he led with the Guiccioli at Genoa, and caused him to remark to Captain Roberts, the builder of his yacht 'The Bolivar',—"Well Captain, if we do not go to Greece, I am determined to go somewhere, and hope we shall all be at sea together by next month, as I am tired of this place, the shore, and all the people on it."[2]

Jeaffreson writes in enumerating the conclusions to be drawn from the different reports of Byron's last moments, that the poet "made no effort to send a message to Teresa Guiccioli. Her name did not come to his lips."[3]

This conclusion is by no means certain. All the reports of Byron's death were made by uneducated Englishmen, with the exception of the strictly medical ones. If Byron had spoken of the Countess, it would most probably have been in Italian, of which language he was so perfect a master, and which he spoke frequently when in delirium on his death

---

[1] That Byron's tendency to obesity was by no means on the wane, at least as late as the summer of 1822, may be seen by consulting Leigh Hunt's work 'Lord Byron and some of his Contemporaries'. vol. 1, pp. 115, 16.

[2] Trelawny's 'Recollections of the Last Days of Shelley and Byron.' London, 1858, p. 161.

[3] 'The Real Lord Byron', standard ed. p. 412.

bed.[1] The uneducated Parry and Byron's valet Fletcher, with their incompetence to understand the signification of whatsoever was said in any language but their own, could not have understood him had he said anything referring to the Countess in one of his frequent attacks of delirium in Italian. Besides there is no evidence whatever that Tita (Byron's Venetian gondolier and afterwards his servant in Italy and Greece), who was much with the dying man, either wrote an account, or gave any of those who did write on the subject, information as regards what the poet said in his hearing in Italian, during his last illness.[2]

Count Gamba, to whom Byron would have been more inclined to converse with on any subject referring to that gentleman's sister, than anyone else, was not near Byron but for a moment during the last days of the poet's life, when he was unable to refrain from weeping at the sight of his friend and was forced to leave the room to prevent Byron's being affected by his display of emotion.

A part of the correspondence between the Countess Guiccioli and Byron, which has not yet been published, will, according to what the Countess (then Marquise de Boissy) said to an American lady,[3] be given to the world fifty years after her death [1923].[1]

---

[1] See Count Gamba's 'Narrative of Lord Byron's last Journey to Greece'. London, 1825, pp. 261, 264;—or 'The Last Days of Lord Byron' by William Parry. London, 1825, p. 124.

[2] Possibly Count Gamba got his information of Byron's having said 'Jo luscio qualche cosa di caro nel mondo' from Tita. See Gamba's 'Narrative' p. 265.

[3] See 'Victoria Magazine' for November 1873, p. 23. As regards what appears to have been another portion of this correspondence, see 'Revue des Deux Mondes' pour le 15 Janvier 1882, p. 301.

[1] The Countess died in March 1873 at Florence.

IX.

Preliminary Intercourse between Byron, Shelley and Leigh Hunt as regards the editing of a projected Journal afterwards called 'The Liberal'.

Byron first met Leigh Hunt in Horsemonger Lane Gaol, whither he was accompanied by Moore, in May 1813,[1] and from that period till Hunt's release from gaol, saw him there on several occassions, treating him with great kindness and making him presents of books and game. From the time of Hunt's release from prison, in February 1815, till Byron left England in April 1816, they saw but little of each other, enough however to enable Byron to describe Hunt to Moore in a letter written at Venice on June 1st 1818, as "a great coxcomb and a very vulgar person in everything about him."[2]

Shelley, who had not yet made Leigh Hunt's acquaintance when he left England on his way to meet Byron in the spring of 1816, had written him a letter of congratulation as editor of the 'Examiner' from University College, Oxford, on the occasion of the brothers Hunt being declared "Not guilty" of libel in March 1811.[3]

When the Hunt's were sentenced to two years imprisonment in February 1813, Shelley wrote to the Old Bond Street publisher Hookam, that he was "boiling over with indignation at the horrible injustice and tyranny of the sentence pronounced

---

[1] Moore was mistaken in giving June 1813, as the date of this meeting. ('*Moore's Life*' etc. 1 vol. ed. p. 183); See Hunt's letter of May 25th 1813 to his wife in 'The Correspondence of Leigh Hunt' edited by his eldest son Thornton Hunt. London, 1862.

[2] 'Moore's Life' etc. letter 317.

[3] Dowden's 'Life of Shelley' vol. 1, p. 113.

on Hunt and his brother," and offred to send twenty pounds wherewith to begin a subscription in their behalf.[1]

After returning from Geneva in the autumn of 1816, Shelley called on Hunt, and their acquaintance had ripened into friendship before the close of that year. The day after Shelley heard of his first wife's suicide, on the 16th of December 1816, he wrote to his mistress from London, — "Leigh Hunt has been with me all day, and his delicate and tender attentions to me, and kind speeches of you, have sustained me against the weight of the horror of this event."[2]

A passage in the second Mrs. Shelley's letter of October 5th 1817 to her husband, will serve to illustrate the intimacy existing between the needy man of letters and the baronet's son at that period. Mrs. Shelley writes, — ',I have written to Hunt; but tell him over and above, that our piano is in tune, and that I wish he would come down by Monday's coach to play me a few tunes. He will think I jest, but it would really give me the greatest pleasure. I would make love to him *pour passer le temps*, that he might not regret the company of his Marianne [*Mrs. Hunt*] and Thornton [*Hunt's eldest son*].[3]

On March 11th 1818, Shelley, Shelley's second wife, their two children, Claire, Allegra and the Swiss nurse Elise, were on the road to Dover on their way to Italy, where they intended having Allegra handed over to her father at Venice, with Hunt's last volume of poetry in their keeping as a present from the author to Byron.

Shelley had not been a fortnight absent from England when he wrote to Hunt from Lyons, — "When shall I see you again? Oh that it might be in Italy! I confess that the thought of how long we may be divided makes me very

---

[1] Dowden's 'Life of Shelley', vol. 1, pp. 324, 25.
[2] Dowden's 'Life of Shelley', vol. 2, p. 68.
[3] Dowden's 'Life of Shelley', vol. 2, p. 148.

melancholy."[1] Hunt replies an the 24th of April of the same year, — "When you write to Lord Byron, pray, remember me particularly to him. Oh! for some of your Italian sunshine ...., to make a proper April with."[2]

As Byron had made a proposition to Moore of being joint editor of a journal with him, as early as January 1817,[3] Shelley, who was no doubt duly affected by Hunt's longing for Italian sunshine, had but little difficulty in persuading Byron to invite Hunt to Italy. It is possible, though highly improbable,[4] that he did no more in 1818 than mention Hunt's desire to come to Italy to Byron who, immediately invited the author of Rimini to do so; probably with the same end in view which he had in inviting him to come to Pisa three years later.

Shelley wrote to his friend Peacock from Naples on December 22nd 1818 — "You don't see much of Hunt. I wish you could contrive to see him when you go up to town, and ask him what he means to answer to Lord Byron's invitation. He has now an opportunity of seeing Italy."[5]

Although Hunt did not accept Byron's invitation in 1818, Byron did not give up the idea of having some kind of periodical publication under his control, and made a second proposition to Moore on the same subject in December 1820.[6]

In the autumn of 1820 Leigh Hunt became seriously ill, and was obliged to discontinue work on the 'Examiner', his brother John was in prison for writing of 'The House of Comons' as 'consisting in the main of public criminals'. Leigh Hunt was at that time the father of six children, and his wife in despair wrote to Mrs. Shelley in January 1821, in referring to Byron, — "Ask

[1] Forman's edition of Shelley's 'Prose Works', vol. 4, p. 4.

[2] 'Correspondence of Leigh Hunt'. London, 1862. vol. 1, p. 118.

[3] 'Moore's Life' etc., letter 259.

[4] See Byron's severely critical remarks on Hunt in his letter to Moore of June 1st 1818, ('Moore's Life' etc., letter 317).

[5] Forman's edition of Shelley's Prose Works', vol. 4, p. 70.

[6] 'Moore's Life' etc., letter 403.

M^r· Shelley *my dear Mrs. Shelley to urge it to him* . . . . . Surely we might sell all our furniture and come over to you." [1]

It seems certain that Byron did not send his first invitation to Hunt in 1818 altogether of his own free will, and that he was influenced in so doing by Shelley; as almost three months before Shelley visited him at Venice, he wrote to Moore on June 1st 1818, in the same letter in which he describes Hunt as 'a very vulgar person', of the same gentleman's last published volume of poetry 'Foliage' thus: "Of all the ineffable Centaurs that were ever begotten by Self-love upon a Night-mare, I think this monstrous Sagittary the most prodigious." [2] It is difficult to conceive that even his tenderness for Hunt, who had taken his part in the 'Examiner' at the time of his separation from his wife, would have prompted Byron to select as a literary partner, a man of whose ability he possessed so low an opinion.

No doubt one of Shelley's reasons [3] for visiting Byron in August 1811 at Ravenna, was to *urge* on the author of Don Juan the project of having Hunt come to Italy for editorial purposes; and though he wrote to Hunt shortly after his return to Pisa, "He [*Byron*] proposes that you should come and go shares with him and me, in a periodical work, to be conducted here," [4] there can be but little doubt but that Shelley had something to do with bringing Byron's journalistic scheme back to the great poet's memory, besides being altogether instrumental in Hunt's being chosen as his and Byron's coadjutor for editing the journal. Possibly Shelley went so far as to let Byron know that he was acting solely in Hunt's behalf. This seems at least probable, judging from

---

[1] Dowden's 'Life of Shelley', vol. 2, p. 439.

[2] 'Moore's Life' etc., 5letter 17.

[3] His other motive in travelling to Ravenna was to visit Allegra at Bagna Cavallo for Claire's sake.

[4] Forman's edition of Shelleys 'Prose Works', vol. 4, p. 235; or Hunt's 'Correspondence' vol., 1, p. 170.

4*

Byron's letter of October 9th 1822[1] to Murray, in which he wrote to his publisher—"They [*the brothers Hunt*] pressed me to engage in this work, and in an evil hour I consented.[2]

Shelley, in writing to Hunt of Byron's proposition, made the bait which was to bring the needy man of letters with his invalid wife and six children[3] to Italy, as tempting as possible; he wrote—"There can be no doubt that the *profits* of any scheme in which you and Lord Byron engage, must, from various, yet cooperating reasons, be very great. As for myself, I am, for the present, only a sort of link between you and him, until you can know each other and effectuate the arrangement; since (to intrust you with a secret which for your sake I withhold from Lord Byron) nothing would induce me to share in the profits,[4] and still less in the borrowed splendour of such a partnership. You and he in different manners would be equal, and would bring, in different manners, but in the same proportion equal stocks of reputation and success."[5]

Hunt, who, at that period of his life, was as vain as a peacock, and 'in the affairs of this world a child',[6] lost his head in reading Shelley's letter and boiled over with pride, hope and ambition.—"What?"—he wrote,—"Are there not

---

[1] 'Moore's Life' etc., letter 504.

[2] Jeaffreson in 'The Real Lord Byron' (standard edition, p. 359) referring to the above letter and letter 509 of 'Moore's Life' etc., writes that in them "Byron talked wide of the truth without knowing it" as regards his relationship with the Hunts in the affair of 'The Liberal'. He is possibly acquainted with some as yet unpublished information on the subject.

[3] Hunt was the father of six children when he left England for Italy. His wife bore him a seventh child on the 8th of June 1823 at Genoa.

[4] Hunt must have inferred from the above, that he would get Shelley's share of the profits of the intended journal besides his own.

[5] Forman's edition of Shelley's 'Prose Works', vol. 4, p. 235.

[6] See Byron's letter to Murray of October 9th 1822 ('Moore's Life' etc., letter 504).

three of us? And ought we not to have as much strength and variety as possible? We will divide the world between us, like the Triumvirate, and you shall be the sleeping partner, if you will; only it shall be with a Cleopatra, and your dreams shall be worth the giving of kingdoms." [1]

When Shelley influenced Byron to invite the very man to Italy, who on one occasion had drawn £ 1400 from his [Shelley's] pocket in one haul, [2] to say nothing of smaller sums, to prey on the author of 'Don Juan', he no longer acted as Byron's friend, but from thence on the relationship between the three men of letters, who were to act as continental editors of the 'Liberal', was a matter of Shelley and Hunt *versus* Byron.

The author of 'Don Juan', who, since 1819, had been cultivating the 'good old-gentlemanly vice', avarice, and lost his temper over the 'inflammation of his weekly bills', assumed an attitude in his commercial dealings in his latter years, almost diametrically opposite to that of Shelley, [3] who till

---

[1] Leigh Hunt's 'Correspodence', vol. I, p. 172.

[2] See 'The Real Shelley', vol. 2, p. 407.

[3] The sharp contrast which existed between Byron's and Shelley's manner of commercial dealing in 1822, may be best illustrated by comparing their respective ways of treating Captain Roberts, the extortionate builder of their yachts, 'The Bolivar' and 'The Don Juan'. Shelley wrote to Trelawny on May 16th 1822, referring to his yacht 'The Don Juan',—"If Robert's £ 50 grow into a £ 500, and his ten days into months, I suppose I may expect that I am considerably in your debt, * *. Whatever may be the result I have little reason and less inclination to complain of my bargain. I wish you could express from me to Roberts, how excessively I am obliged to him for the time and trouble he has expended for my advantage, and which I wish could be as easily repaid as the money which I owe him, and which I wait your orders for remitting" (Forman's edition of Shelley's 'Prose Works', vol. 4, p. 270). In a letter from Williams to Trelawny, published in Trelawny's 'Recollections' (first edition pp. 111, 12), Williams wrote,— "Lord B's reception of Mrs. H. [*Hunt*] was, as S. [*Shelley*] tells me most shameful * *; but the way in which he received our friend Roberts, at Dunn's door, shall be described when we meet:—it must be acted."

his death was a prey to every clever parasite who approached him, and who no doubt thought that Byron should have squandered his money on Hunt, who according to his own statement had 'peculiar notions on the subject of money', and thought the giver should be thankful to the receiver for accepting a pecuniary donation.[1]

One of the reasons which account for Byron's readiness to accept Hunt as his literary partner, was the false impression, under which both he and Shelley laboured, that Leigh Hunt was still joint-proprietor of the 'Examiner'.[2]

Byron had not been long in Pisa when Shelley wrote to Hunt,—"What arrangements have you made about the receipt of a regular income from the profits of the 'Examiner'? You ought not to leave England without having the assurance of an independence in this particular; as many difficulties have presented themselves to the plan imagined by Lord Byron, which I depend upon you for getting rid of."[3]

On March 2nd 1822, Shelley wrote to Hunt,—"He [*Byron*] renews his expressions of disregard for the opinions of those who advised him against this alliance with you, and I imagine it will be no very difficult task to execute that which you have assigned me—to keep him in heart with the project until your arrival, * * *. No feelings of my own shall injure or interfere with what is now nearest to them—your interest, and I will take care to preserve the little influence I may have over this Proteus in whom such strange extremes are reconciled, until we meet."[4]

It is evident from another passage in the same letter, that Byron had become aware that it was Hunt's interest and not that of the author of 'Don Juan' that Shelley had

---

[1] 'Lord Byron and some of his Contemporaries'. Paris, 1828. vol. 1, p. 32

[2] See Trelawny's 'Recollections', first edition, p. 155.

[3] Forman's edition of Shelley's 'Prose Work's, vol. 4, p. 252.

[4] Forman's edition of Shelley's 'Prose Works'. vol. 4. pp. 258 59. 60.

at heart, and had given Shelley to unterstand that he, Byron, was aware of the real state of things. Shelley writes to Hunt,—"Lord Byron shewed me your letter to him, *which arrived with mine*[1] yesterday. How shall I thank you for your generous and delicate defence and explanation of my motives. I fear no misinterpretation from you, and from anyone else I despise and defy it."

While Shelley was at work at the task assigned him by Hunt, keeping Byron 'in heart with the project' of the journal, praising Hunt's literary ability, and painting in roseate hues the commercial soundness of the newspaper enterprise, Byron would no doubt make sarcastic remarks in the 'Don Juan' style to the contrary effect, so as to let his associate poet see that it was not in his nature *d'être dupe* of a man his junior in years and experience.

That Byron must have annoyed Shelley considerably on the subject of Hunt and the projected journal, will appear from a letter of Shelley to John Gisborne, dated June 18th 1822, in which the advocate for the rich emptying their pockets on professional parasites wrote,—"Hunt is not yet arrived, but I expect him every day. I shall see little of Lord Byron, nor shall I permit Hunt to form the intermediate link between him and me. I detest all society—almost all, at least—and Lord Byron is the nucleus of all that is hateful and tiresome in it."[2]

The day after Shelley wrote the letter just quoted, Hunt arrived in Genoa, and Shelley sent him the following note from Lerici: "A thousand welcomes, my best friend, to this divine country; high mountains and seas no longer divide those whose affections are united."[3]

Ten days after Hunt's arrival in Genoa, Shelley, who in the preceeding August, was so exuberantly hopeful as regards the projected newspaper, wrote to Horace Smith,—

---

[1] We have caused the italics to be inserted.

[2] Forman's edition of Shelley's 'Prose Works', vol. 4, p. 279.

[3] Forman's edition of Shelley's 'Prose Works', vol. 4, p. 283.

"Between ourselves, I greatly fear that this alliance will not succeed; for I, who could never have been regarded as more than the link of the two thunderbolts, cannot now consent to be even that; and how long the alliance between the wren and the eagle [1] may continue I will not prophecy." [2]

Not a week after writing the above letter, but four days before his death, on learning of the Gambas being banished from Tuscany and of Byron's having declared his intention of following their fortunes, Shelley wrote to his wife,—"But it is the worse for poor Hunt, unless the present storm should blow over. He places his whole dependence upon this scheme of a journal, for which every arrangement has been made, and arrived with no other remnant of his £ 400 [3] than a debt of 60 crowns. Lord Byron must of course furnish the requisite funds at present as I cannot; but he seems inclined to depart without the necessary explanations and arrangements due to such a situation as Hunt's. This in spite of delicacy I must procure; he offers him the copyright of the Vision of Judgment [1] for his first number. This offer if sincere, is *more* than enough to set up the journal, and if sincere will set everything right." [5]

Hunt, who came to Italy puffed up with the vanity with which Shelley's letter containing Byron's proposal had inspired him, and his 'peculiar notions on the subject of money'. treated the great poet as if he were Byron's literary equal and could be under no obligations to him whatever. The

---

[1] This from the man who had written a few months previously to Hunt,—"You and he [*Byron*] in different manners would be equal etc."

[2] Forman's edition of Shelley's 'Prose Works', vol. 4, p. 286.

[3] Byron lent Shelley £ 200 for Hunt on Shelley's bond, besides which Shelley sent Hunt on one occasion £ 150 out of his own slender income of £ 1000 per annum. I am not aware from what source Hunt obtained the remaining £ 50.

[4] Byron not only gave Hunt 'The Vision of Judgment' *gratis*, but also the 'Letter to the Editor of my Grandmother's Review', 'Heaven and Earth', his translation of the 'Morgante Maggiore', and 'The Blues'.

[5] Forman's edition of Shelley's 'Prose Works', vol. 4, p. 289.

exact nature of Hunt's attitude towards Byron may be best described in the words of the needy journalist himself, who, a quarter of a century after Byron's death, wrote in his 'Autobiography',—"His [*Byron's*] friends in England, who, after what had lately taken place there in his instance, were opposed naturally enough, to his opening new fields of publicity, did what they could to prevent his taking a hearty interest in the 'Liberal'; and I must confess, that I did not mend the matter by my own inability to fall in cordially with his ways, and by a certain jealousy of my position, which prevented me, neither very wisely nor justly, from manifesting the admiration due to his genius, and reading the manuscripts he showed me with a becoming amount of thanks and good words. I think he had a right to feel this want of accord in a companion, whatever might be its value. A dozen years later, reflection would have made me act very differently." [1]

Byron wrote to Moore after it became evident to him that 'The Liberal' would be a failure,—"Think a moment— he [*Leigh Hunt*] is perhaps the vainest man on earth, at least his friends say so pretty loudly; and if he were in other circumstances, I might be tempted to take him down a peg; but not now,—it would be cruel"; and again to the same correspondent,—"I cannot describe to you the despairing sensation of trying to do something for a man who seems incapable or unwilling to do anything further for himself, —at least to the purpose. It is like pulling a man out of a river who directly throws himself in again. For the last three or four years Shelley assisted and had once actually extricated him. [2] I have since his demise,—and even before,

---

[1] 'The Autobiography of Leigh Hunt'. London, 1850, vol. 2, p. 176.

[2] It would seem from the above, that Shelley had imprudently informed Byron to what extent he had assisted Hunt financially, which was no doubt *une raison de plus* for Byron's looking out that this king of parasites got no more money out of his pocket than absolutely necessary.

—done what I could: but it is not in my power to make this permanent."[1]

Another side of Byron's trials with Leigh Hunt and family, besides the vanity and sycophancy of the journalist and the downright rudeness of Mrs. Hunt, he himself describes graphically in a letter written on October 6th 1822 to Mrs. Shelley, as follows: "I have a particular dislike of anything of Shelley's being within the same walls with Mrs. Hunt's children. They are dirtier and more mischievous than Yahoos. What they can't destroy with their filth, they will with their fingers***. Poor Hunt, with his six little blackguards, are coming slowly up, as usual he turned back once—was there ever such a *Kraal* out of the Hottentot country before"?[2,3]

Hunt could not have begun to find any serious fault with Byron's treatment of him, till a few days before immigration from Pisa to Genoa [*Sept. 22nd or 23rd 1822*], as he wrote to Mr. and Mrs. Novello from Pisa on September 9th 1822, —"Lord Byron is very kind".[1] As late as July 1823 [*Byron set sail for Greece on the 17th of July 1823*], Mrs. Shelley writes of Byron "still keeping up an appearance of amity with Hunt."[5]

On the 10th of June 1823, Mrs. Shelley (the expenses of whose return to England Lord Byron had promised to defray) told Byron she was ready to return to her native country, and in a letter just quoted[6] wrote to Jane Williams —"He [*Byron*] chose to transact our negociation through

[1] 'Moore's Life' etc., letter 511.
[2] 'The Life and Letters of Mary Wollstonecraft Shelley', vol. 2, p. 46.
[3] Trelawny writes: "Hunt's theory and practice were that children should be unrestrained until they were of an age to be reasoned with. See Trelawny's Records ed. of 1887, p. 117.
[4] 'Recollections of Writers' by Charles and Mary Cowden Clarke. London, 1878, p. 218.—Hunt also wrote to his wife's sister on July 20th 1822, of Lord Byron's kindness—See 'Correspondence of Leigh Hunt', vol. 1, p. 190.
[5] 'Life and Letters of Mary Wollstonecraft Shelley', vol. 2, p. 80.
[6] Dated July 1823.

Hunt, and gave such an air of unwillingness and sense of the obligation he conferred, as at last provoked Hunt to say that there was no obligation, since he owed me £ 1000;[1] also—"You would laugh at his last letter to Hunt, when he says concerning his connection with Shelley 'that he let himself down to the level of the democrats'."[2]

Both Mrs. Shelley and Leigh Hunt wrote kindly of Byron on hearing of his death.

Mrs. Shelley wrote,—"Can I forget his attentions and consolations to me during my deepest misery?—Never!"

"Beauty sat on his countenance and power beamed from his eye. His faults being, for the most part, weaknesses, induced one readily to pardon them."

"Albé[3]—the dear capricious, fascinating Albé—has left this desert world."[4]

Hunt wrote,—"I could not help feeling emotion at the news of Lord B's death, strange as his conduct was. Poor fellow! he was the most spoilt of men; and I do believe was naturally good."[5]

But four years had passed since penning the above lines, when Hunt published his base and vulgar work on Byron; beyond all odds the most vile and lying book ever written on a man of equal genius.

---

[1] Probably referring to a bet of £ 1000 made by Byron to Shelley that Sir Timothy Shelley would die before Lady Noel;—see Medwin's 'Life of Shelley', vol. 2, p. 243.

[2] 'Life and Letters of Mary Wollstonecraft Shelley', vol. 2, p. 80.

[3] Probably derived from L. B. (Lord Byron), or Albanian.

[4] Mrs. Shelley's diary for May 15th 1824, in 'The Life and Letters of Mary Wollstonecraft Shelley', vol. 2, p. 113.

[5] Leigh Hunt's 'Correspondence', vol. 1, p. 222.

Vita.

On the 24th of November, 1866, I was born in New York City. I received my collegiate education at the Pennsylvania Military College where I graduated in the summer of 1885. In the autumn of 1887 I matriculated in Leipzig, where during the last five years, with the exception of the year 1890 and the closing months of 1889 when I soujourned in Paris, I heard the lectures of Professors Wülker, Adolf Birch-Hirschfeld, Zarncke, Maurenbrecher, Biedermann, von Bahder, Marshall, Elster, and of Dr. Witkowski and Dr. Flügel. To all of these exellent teachers I am much indebted. To Professor Wülker especially, I desire to express my obligation for valuable help and kind advice.